# Moby - Dick: A Quick Play

## By: C.S. Zheng

## Based on the novel by : Herman Melville

ISBN-13: 978-0692905388
ISBN-10: 0692905383

# Moby - Dick
## Cast:
### (In order of appearance)

 Tom Mittens as:
Ishmael, a young school teacher looking for whales and adventure.

 Pawlick Furwin as:
Captain Ahab, Captain of the Pequod with one goal: to hunt down the White Whale.

 John Tabby as:
Innkeeper, owner of the Spouter Inn.

 Felix Gravel as:
Queequeg, an expert harpooner from the South Pacific.

 Percy Sandbox as:
Starbuck, first mate of the Pequod.

 Kit Arrow as:
Tashtego, a Native American whaler.

 Spike Cuddles as:
Daggoo, a prince from an African village who voluntarily joined a whale ship.

**Ishmael:**

Call me Ishmael.
Feeling gloomy, I'll set sail.
I'll join a ship out to sea to catch a great whale.

**Ishmael:**

But before I go,
The night is cold.
Excuse me innkeeper,
Have you a room to spare?

**Innkeeper:**

We're all full,
Unless you share.

**Ishmael:**

Share a room with a stranger?

**Innkeeper:**

He is strange...
But not a danger.

**Ishmael:**

Seeing my roommate for the night
Gave me quite a fright!

**Queequeg:**
Me Queequeg.
I hear you go whaling too.
I share my bed.
We friends be true.

**Ishmael:**

My new friend, let's ship together
For fun and adventure
In this ark sturdy and broad
Called the Pequod.
Their captain many praise highly.
Ignore those who say he's crazy.

**Starbuck:** Ahoy landlubbers!
I'm first mate Starbuck.
I wish ye all luck.
Whaling is a tall order.
We hunt them for their blubber;
That's oil used to light your shelter.
But enough of my gab,
Here comes Captain Ahab!

**Ahab:**

Ahoy! Gather ye on deck
To hear my tale.
Last at sea, I was nearly shipwrecked
And lost my leg to a fearsome white whale!

**Queequeg:**
Captain, me know this fishy.
His name be Moby Dick.

**Ahab:**
Aye, that be he:
Vicious, tricky, and quick!
Will ye join me
For revenge and glory?

**Starbuck:**

Oh Captain, hear my plea.
A provoked beast is not thine bitter enemy.
Your hatred for one whale
May cause our mission to fail.

**Ahab:**

Quiet your fear!
This here gold doubloon
Goes to he who shouts a tune
When Moby Dick appear!

**Crew:**

Huzza! Huzza!

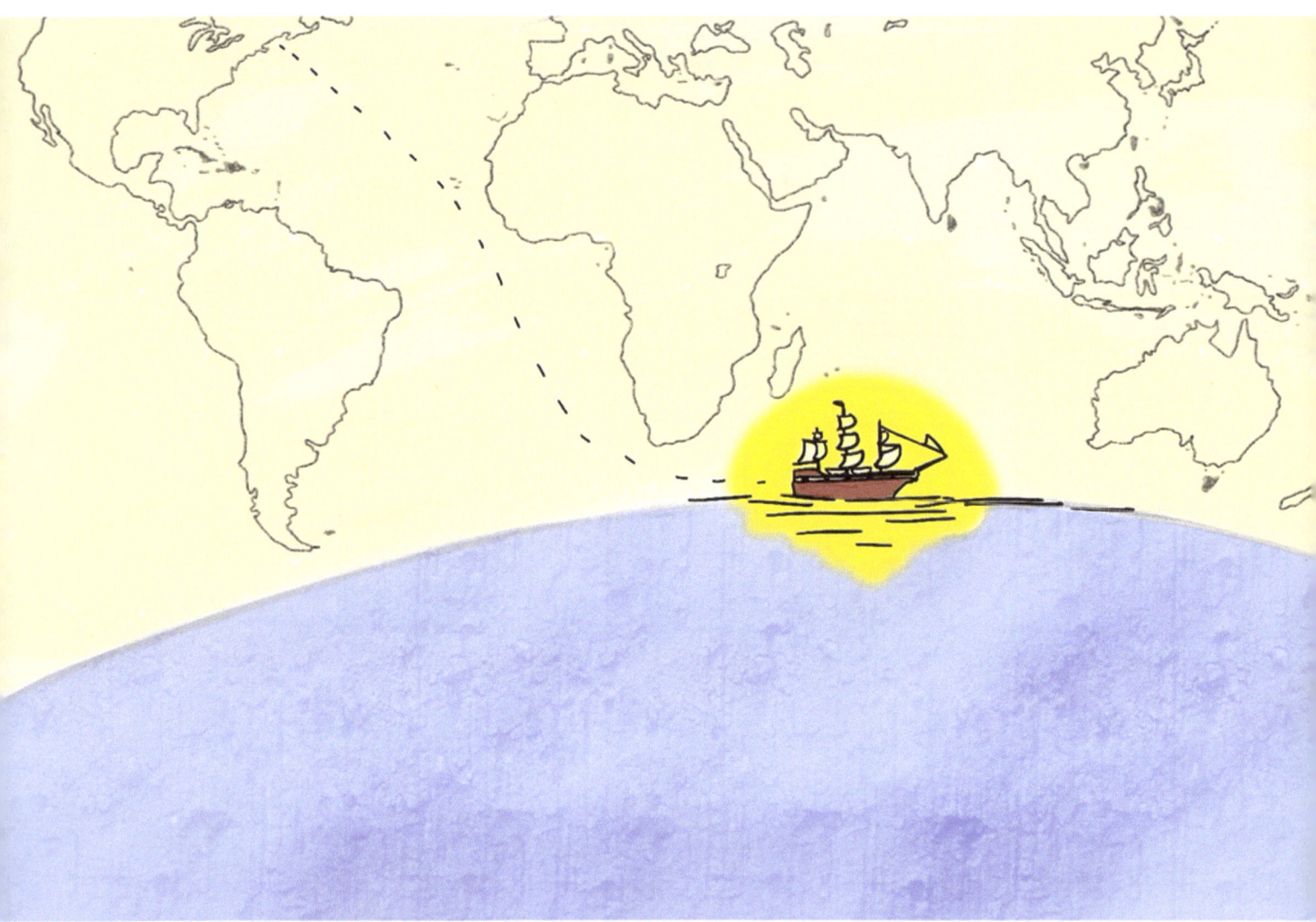

**Ishmael:**

For many months we searched,
Encountering great mammoths of the sea.

**Tashtego:**
Ahoy, a blue whale!

**Ahab:**
The whale I seek is white!

**Daggoo**
To the left, a right whale!

**Ahab:**
Nay, wrong whale!

**Ishmael:**

Hark, a school of dolphins!

**Ahab:**

Waste not my time boy.
Focus on our purpose!

**Starbuck:**

Captain, a storm is brewing.
Wind, thunder, and lightning
Will split and flip our ship!

**Ahab:**

I be not afraid of thunder and gale.
The white fires of the sky light the way to my whale!

**Queequeg:**
Captain, there.

**Ahab:**
Aye, there she blows!
Go! Go! Go!
To your boats!
Row! Row! Row!

**Ahab:**

Faster! Faster!
Get me closer!

**Ahab:**
Oh no...
The ship!!!

**Starbuck:**

Oh dear.

**Narrator:**
Unnatural anger
Against a force of nature
Ends in disaster.

# Epilogue

**Old Man:**
Hi there!

# Cetology: Whale Facts

First off, whales are big. Really big. The blue whale is the largest animal on Earth. They can grow to 98 feet in length (an adult person is about 5-6 feet tall) and weigh over 200 tons (a car is about 1-2 tons). Meanwhile, a sperm whale is the largest toothed animal and are about half the size of blue whales (blue, like other baleen whales, have no teeth).

Moby Dick is a sperm whale. He was based on a real white sperm whale called Mocha Dick that was attacked by over 100 ships and destroyed around 20 from 1810 to 1838. Mocha Dick was 70 ft long and didn't attack ships unless provoked. He would swim peacefully along friendly ships and only attacked ships when they attacked him or other whales.

Whalers often named deadly whales based on the location they were first spotted along with a common male name. For instance: Mocha Dick, Timor Jack, or New Zealand Tom.

Whales are not actually fish, but mammals like lions, bears, horses, or people. Fish are cold blooded, can breath under water, and lay eggs. Whales are warm blooded, need to surface to breathe air, and don't lay eggs.

Different whale species have different blowholes which are used for breathing. Experienced whalers could distinguish the type of whale by its spout. Sperm whales have blowholes on the left side so their spout sprays to the left. Baleen whales have 2 blowholes.

That's about all I know of whales, which is not much. Whales are fascinating creatures and we may never learn all there is to know. What will you discover?

# Stage Your World And Play!

Follow the script or take the story in new and exciting directions!

www.ingramcontent.com/pod-product-compliance
Lightning Source LLC
Chambersburg PA
CBHW041608120626
46551CB00002B/354